Three Foolish Sisters

by
W.G. Van de Hulst

illustrated by
Willem G. Van de Hulst, Jr.

**INHERITANCE PUBLICATIONS
NEERLANDIA, ALBERTA, CANADA
PELLA, IOWA, U.S.A.**

Library and Archives Canada Cataloguing in Publication
Hulst, W. G. van de (Willem Gerrit), 1879-1963
[Van drie domme zusjes. English]
    Three foolish sisters / by W.G. Van de Hulst ; illustrated by
Willem G. Van de Hulst, Jr. ; [translated by Harry der Nederlanden].
(Stories children love ; 15)
Translation of: Van drie domme zusjes.
Originally published: St. Catharines, Ontario : Paideia Press, 1980.
ISBN 978-1-928136-15-6 (pbk.)
    I. Hulst, Willem G. van de (Willem Gerrit), 1917-, illustrator
II. Nederlanden, Harry der, translator III. Title. IV. Title: Van drie
dome zusjes. English V. Series: Hulst, W. G. van de (Willem Gerrit),
1879-1963 Stories children love ; 15
PZ7.H873985Thre 2014   j839.313'62   C2014-903608-6

Library of Congress Cataloging-in-Publication Data
Hulst, W. G. van de (Willem Gerrit), 1879-1963.
[Van drie domme zusjes. English.]
Three foolish sisters / by W.G. Van de Hulst ; illustrated by Willem G. Van de Hulst, Jr. ;
edited by Paulina Janssen.
pages cm. — (Stories children love ; #15)
"Originally published in Dutch as Van drie domme zusjes. Original translation done by
Harry der Nederlanden for Paideia Press, St. Catharines-Ontario-Canada."
Summary: Sisters Dinah, Suzy, and Joanne are playing in the woods, practically ignoring
their baby brother Joey, but when he winds up on the other side of the large iron gate
leading to dark, scary woods surrounding the Baron's estate, they must conquer their fear
and get him out.
ISBN 978-1-928136-15-6
[1. Brothers and sisters—Fiction. 2. Lost children—Fiction. 3. Fear—Fiction. 4.
Behavior—Fiction.] I. Hulst, Willem G. van de (Willem Gerrit), 1917- illustrator. II.
Title.
PZ7.H887Thr 2014   [E]—dc23   2014017992

Originally published in Dutch as *Van drie domme zusjes*
Cover painting and illustrations by Willem G. Van de Hulst, Jr.
Original translation done by Harry der Nederlanden for Paideia Press,
St. Catharines-Ontario-Canada.
The publisher expresses his appreciation to John Hultink of Paideia Press for
his generous permission to use his translation (ISBN 0-88815-515-8).

Edited by Paulina Janssen

ISBN 978-1-928136-15-6

Published simultaneously in U.S.A. by Inheritance Publications
Box 366, Pella, Iowa 50219

Printed in Canada

Contents

1. Little Brother

Cheep-cheep!
A little baby bird sat on the path. He spread his little wings wide as if he wanted to fly. He opened his little beak wide too as if he wanted something to eat. Cheep-cheep!

5

The path ran along the woods. It was very quiet. No one saw the baby bird.

Along the quiet path stood a high wall. It was very old and crooked. In the wall was an iron gate. It was always closed. On it hung a heavy iron chain and a big padlock.
But on top of the wall . . . ?
Cheep-cheep!
The little bird chirped and chirped. He was lonely. And he was hungry too.
On top of the wall were three more baby birds. They were his sisters. They were playing.
In the wall were dark crannies where they could hide.

6

And there were lots of mosquitoes and spiders and bugs for them to eat. They were having great fun.

They did not see their little brother sitting on the path below even though they had pushed him off. They had not noticed. And their little brother could not fly.

Those foolish little sisters! Oh, if their father found out . . . If their mother saw it . . .

Cheep-cheep!

2. Come and See

Listen! There were children in the woods. Listen to them laugh and shout. They were coming. They were coming down the quiet path. Then the quiet path was no longer quiet.

They were three sisters and their little brother. The little boy was very young. He rode in a wagon. He thought he could talk pretty well, but he really couldn't. Oh, no!

Dinah was the oldest. She was making most of the noise.

Joanne was the quietest. She was pulling the wagon.

Little Suzy was the wildest. She ran up and down the path like a puppy. First she darted here, then there.

No, the quiet path was no longer quiet.

The poor little bird became frightened — very frightened. He fluttered his wings and scrambled away on his tiny feet. He hid in the tall grass along the wall.

He hopped into the air. But the wall was too high — much too high. He hopped again . . . and again. His feet scratched at the wall. The noise on the path was coming closer. Huge, towering creatures were coming down the path. The little bird shivered with fear.

He stuck his head deep into a hole in the wall — deep into the darkness. He no longer dared to chirp. He did not even dare look.

Little Suzy darted past. She did not see the little bird.

But all at once she stopped.

Her eyes sparkled. And yet, at the same time, she also looked a little frightened. She waved to the others and called to them very softly, "Come here! Come and see!"

Dinah ran to Suzy. "What? What is it?"

Dinah did not see the little bird either.

Joanne trotted along behind her pulling the wagon. "What? What is it?"

Joanne did not see the little bird either. She was too busy watching Joey and the wagon.

Suzy pointed to the iron gate. Well, look at that! That was strange! The chain was loose and the big gate was standing open — just a little. The big gate had never been open before. Never!

But now it was. One side was still closed but the other was open — just a little. How strange!

The three sisters had always been a little frightened of the big iron gate. Behind it were dark woods with trees and shrubs and winding paths. And it was always very quiet and spooky in those woods. You couldn't help become a little frightened when you peeked through the gate.

Do you know what they did sometimes?

They would put their heads between the thick iron bars and then they would shout, "BOO!" very loud. "BOOO!"

Oh, that would send cold shivers down their backs. Then they would run away and they

would feel as if all kinds of hairy creatures were coming after them. That was such fun! But they were not just pretending. They really were a little frightened of what lived in the dark woods behind the big iron gate.

But now the gate was standing open. How strange! How eerie!

They whispered very softly. It seemed so
strange.

Being the oldest, Dinah was also the boldest.
She went closer to take a better look.

She stuck her head through the open gate. But
that still wasn't bold enough. She climbed onto
the loose gate. It swung a little. That was fun.

Oh, but suddenly wild little Suzy ran up behind
her. Thump! She gave Dinah a shove. Suzy
squealed in delight.

But poor Dinah swung inward on the big iron gate. Squeak-squeak! went the gate. Dinah squealed in fright. She fled, terrified.

Suzy was already running.

Joanne ran too, the wagon bouncing along behind her. Joey tumbled backward, his legs in the air.

Oh, what if those hairy creatures came after them?

But the three frightened sisters did not run very far.

Not at all! Soon they stopped.

Dinah scolded Suzy, "You meanie!" But then she laughed.

They all laughed.

Joey scrambled up in the wagon again. He squealed in delight, "Joey go boom! Joey go boom!"

"Let's go back and take another look," said Dinah.

"I'm scared!" said Joanne.

"I'm not!" said little Suzy. And she started back.

She tiptoed forward, her hands on her back.

The iron gate was now standing wide open.
Oh, Suzy's eyes sparkled with excitement.
"Come on!" she called softly. "Come on!"

3. Red Berries

Look! There they went, those three foolish
sisters. Yes, there they went right into the dark
woods. First they went just a little
ways, and then a little farther, and
then . . . ?
How did they dare!

Little Suzy went first.
She tiptoed forward, her
hands on her back. She
bit her lips in fear but

her eyes sparkled with excitement. The naughty little rascal.

And Dinah stepped inside too. She did not want to look scared.

Joanne was frightened. And Joanne had to pull the wagon.

Little Joey was not frightened at all. He wanted to go with Dinah. "Joey too! Joey too!" he cried. He rocked the wagon eagerly.

Then Joanne started forward too — just a little ways. She was right by the gate.

Dinah spotted something in the grass.

Look! Over there! Hundreds of red berries.

She bent down. They were strawberries. Tiny strawberries. They were growing wild in the grass.

Dinah picked one. She tasted it. Then she picked another . . . and another. Mmm! They were good!

Suzy quickly joined her. She knelt in the grass.
And she tasted too. Mmm! Good!

"What did you find?" cried Joanne.
"Come on!" called Dinah. "Come and see!"
Suzy ran back to the wagon. In her hand she
clutched two strawberries — one for Joanne
and one for Joey. "This one's for you!" she
said and stuffed one red berry into Joanne's
hand. "And this one's for you!" she said and
stuffed the other red berry in Joey's mouth.
Oh, but then Joey became wild with excitement.
"Joey more candy! Joey more candy!" When
Suzy ran back, he screamed even louder. "Joey
more candy! Joey more candy!" He almost fell
out of the wagon in excitement.

Joanne also tasted the little red berry. Mmm!
Good! She wanted to go and pick the little red

berries too. She went forward a little farther. She shuffled through the gate. She shuffled a little farther . . . still farther . . .

Soon Joanne was also picking. She had already found two, three . . . five berries. Joey held his mouth wide open — just like a baby bird. And Joanne stuffed the red berries inside. All five of them. Mmm! Good!

But she still felt a little frightened. "Are you sure it's all right for us to pick them?" she asked.

"Of course!" said Dinah. "They're not real strawberries. They're only wild ones. It's all right."

Joanne was still a little frightened.

The dark woods belonged to the Baron. He was a very important man with a long, white beard. He always looked very proud and proper. His house had two large towers and was very, very large. It was a castle. But you couldn't see it from here. Not at all. It was far away from the gate. Here it was very quiet. There was no one here but them.

Joanne thought, "What if the Baron sees us here?"

Little Suzy was not frightened at all. She went farther and farther into the woods. She called, "Dinah, come here! There are lots and lots of them over here! Come and see!"

She knelt in the grass and picked with both hands. She picked lots and lots of them. Dinah also went farther and farther into the woods. A little farther all the time.

And Joanne . . . ? Soon she forgot her fears. Little Joey bounced up and down in the wagon. "Joey more! Joey more!" And Joanne pulled him across the grass, past the bushes, into the middle of the strawberry patch.

Those foolish sisters!

4. Crunch, Crunch!

Crunch . . . crunch!
What was that? Joanne stopped and listened. No, she no longer heard it. So she went on picking strawberries.

Through the woods ran a dry gully. Suzy scrambled through it. Dinah jumped over it. But Joanne could not pull the wagon across it.

"Dinah!" she cried. "Dinah, come back!" But Dinah didn't come back. She put all her strawberries in her apron — for Mother. Little Suzy put all her strawberries in her apron too — also for Mother.

"Dinah, come back! Suzy, come back!" But Dinah did not come back. She kept on picking. Suzy did come back. She ran back, her apron filled with berries. She scrambled through the gully. Oh, look, her strawberries were falling out of her apron.

"Now you can look after Joey for a while!" grumbled Joanne. "Then I can pick strawberries too — for Mother. Watch him close, Suzy. You hear? Don't leave him alone! "

Joanne crossed the gully and disappeared into the bushes. Suzy stayed with Joey. She would watch Joey very closely.

"Look, Joey, look how many I've got!" But when she looked in her apron, she saw only a few. How could that be? She had only a handful left. Where had all the others gone?

Suzy put them in the wagon — in one corner. "Don't eat them, Joey! You hear? Don't eat them! I'm going to pick some more. Some for you too. But Joey must stay here! Suzy will be right back."

18

Suzy scrambled back through the gully and disappeared into the bushes.

Where had Dinah gone? Where had Joanne gone?

But Suzy wasn't really looking for *them*. No, she was looking for more of those delicious strawberries.

Those foolish girls! One wandered this way; the other that way. Soon they had lost track of one another.

Crunch . . . crunch . . . crunch!

What was that? Joanne stopped to listen.

She saw nothing. But she *did* hear something. It was coming closer!

Crunch . . . crunch . . . crunch!

Joanne became frightened. "Dinah! Dinah!" she cried. But she did not see Dinah anywhere. Crunch . . . crunch . . . crunch! Oh, Joanne was very frightened. She crept out of the bushes. But she was not sure which way it was to Joey and the wagon. She stumbled onto a path. Crunch!

Oh, how terrible! A man came pushing a wheelbarrow. The wheelbarrow squeaked. The man saw her. Angrily he grumbled, "What are you doing here?"

Joanne fled. She raced down one path and then down another. Suddenly ahead of her she saw the gate. Oh, what a relief! The gate — the open gate!

She fled through the gate onto the quiet path and into the bushes on the other side. She did not even dare look back. Poor Joanne!

And Dinah? Where was Dinah?

Dinah heard the deep voice grumble, "What are you doing here?"

It frightened her. Quickly she crept out of the bushes. Oh, how terrible! She almost bumped into a wheelbarrow! Behind it stood a man — a man with huge, brown hands. And those hands were reaching for her.

"No! No!" she screamed and fled. She raced down one path and then another. Suddenly ahead of her she saw the gate. Oh, what a relief! The gate — the open gate!

She fled through the gate onto the quiet path and into the bushes on the other side. She hid behind a big tree and covered her eyes with her hands. She did not even dare to peek around the side. She was too frightened. Poor Dinah!

And little Suzy? Where was Suzy?

Suzy was picking strawberries — lots and lots of them. Suddenly she heard something too.

She looked around but she saw nothing. What was that? Oh, how terrible!

A man burst through the bushes. "What's this?" he grumbled. "Another little trespasser?"

"Oh, no, no!" screamed Suzy, throwing up her hands. All her pretty strawberries spilled into the grass.

As he reached for Suzy, the man's pants snagged on a branch. He missed. Suzy fled, out of the bushes, down the path.

"No, no!" she screamed as she ran down another path. Suddenly ahead of her she saw the gate. Oh, what a relief! The gate — the open gate!

She fled through the gate onto the quiet path. She ran on until she tripped over her own feet and sprawled in the sand.

"Oh, no!" she screamed. On her hands and knees, she crawled under a big bush. She did not even dare to look up. Two big tears spilled down her cheeks into the sand. She was terribly frightened. Poor Suzy!

Crunch . . . crunch . . . crunch!
The wheelbarrow rolled up to the iron gate. The gardener grumbled to himself. He looked down the quiet path but he saw no one.

Then he closed the gate, wrapped the heavy chain around it, and snapped on the padlock. He pushed his wheelbarrow back into the woods.

Then it was quiet again on the path. But against the old wall sat a frightened little bird.
What if a hungry cat came by?
What if some nasty children spotted him?

His three playful sisters had forgotten all about him.
His mother did not know he was there.
And neither did his father.
They were out looking for food for the four baby birds.
Cheep, cheep!

5. The Gate

Little Suzy peered from under the big bush. The scary man was gone. Her fright was going away too.
She stood up. Where was Joanne? And Dinah? And Joey? Were they still in the dark woods behind the gate?
She tiptoed forward. She would go and see. Had that man also seen Dinah and Joanne and Joey?

Dinah peeked around the side of the big tree. Her fright was going away. She crept back to the quiet path. Ah, there was Suzy. But where was Joanne? And Joey? Were they still in the dark woods behind the gate?

Had that angry man also seen Joanne and Joey?

Suzy whispered, "Come on, let's go back and take a look."

Oh, look, look!
There came Joanne.
But where was Joey?
A sudden, horrible fright seized the girls. They were all here — all three of them. But where . . . where was Joey?
Joanne ran up to Suzy. "Suzy, where is Joey? You promised to look after him."
But Suzy suddenly began to cry. "I don't know!" she sobbed.
The three foolish girls looked at one another. Their hearts pounded in fear. Where could Joey be?

Dinah was the oldest. She was also the wisest. "Follow me!" she said. "Follow me! We'll go
24

get him. Oh, if Mother knew! Come on, let's hurry. I'm glad that terrible man is gone. Come, let's go back through the gate."

She broke into a run. Suzy ran after her. So did Joanne. They no longer thought of the angry man. They thought only of Joey who was lost. Poor little Joey!

They ran along the wall.
The little bird went, "Cheep, cheep!"
But the three girls did not hear him.
They ran toward the gate.
They could see it already.
They were almost there . . .

"Oh . . . !"

Dinah grabbed the bars. She pulled, she tugged, she pushed. The chain rattled but the gate stayed shut.

"Oh, Joey! Joey!" she cried.

And Little Suzy climbed up on the gate. "Joey! Joey!"

And Joanne squeezed between Dinah and Suzy. "Joey! Joey! Jo-o-ey!"

They all stuck their heads between the bars and shouted and screamed and sobbed. But they

25

heard nothing . . . nothing . . . nothing at all.
Oh, what now? What now . . . ?

Those three foolish sisters! What could they
do? They had lost their little brother. And it
was all their own fault!
Oh, if Mother knew! If Father found out!
Poor little Joey!

6. "Follow Me!"

"Let's go," sobbed little Suzy. "Let's go, Joanne." She tugged at Joanne's apron. Big tears tumbled down her cheeks. "Come on, Joanne, let's go tell Mother!"

Joanne wiped away her tears with her apron. But the apron was covered with red spots from the strawberries she had picked. They made Joanne's nose red too — strawberry red.

"I know what we'll do!" cried Dinah. "Oh, yes, I know!"

"What? What?"

Dinah talked very softly. And the three little sisters put their heads close together.

Suzy whispered, "Aren't you afraid?"

And Joanne whispered, "Are you sure it's all right?"

But Dinah said, "Just follow me. I know a place. Follow me!"

They walked along the wall — in a big hurry. Suzy had to trot to keep up because her legs were so short. They walked until there was no wall anymore. There was only a deep ditch with sloping sides and water in the bottom. On the other side of the ditch were the dark woods.

"I know a place. Right here. This is the place."
Dinah scrambled down the bank till she was
close to the water. Then . . . thump! She leaped
to the other side.

"No, no!" cried Joanne. "I'm afraid!"

But Suzy also scrambled down the bank. She
leaped too. Splash! Oh, her legs were too short.
Her feet landed in the water.

"Oh, no, no!" cried Joanne. "I can't! I'm
afraid!"

Suzy was already scrambling up the other bank.
Her shoes were caked with black mud. Big tears
sprang to her eyes. But she did not cry. She
wiped off her shoes with her handkerchief. Now
her handkerchief was black too.

Dinah shouted, "Come on, Joanne! Jump!"

At last Joanne overcame her fear. She leaped
as far as she could. Thump! She made it with
room to spare. Now they were all on the other
side.

The three little girls hurried into the dark
woods. They followed a path and crossed a
little footbridge.

Softly they called, "Joey! Jo-o-ey!"

They searched the bushes; they searched
everywhere. But they found no trace of Joey.

Oh, they became very frightened and very sad.
They began to cry — all three of them.
Poor little sisters!

7. The Dark Woods

The three sisters wandered about in the woods.
But they did not know where they were going.
And little Joey was nowhere to be found.
Suddenly . . .

"Oh, look, look! Over there!"
Far ahead of them someone was walking along
the path. It was a man with a white beard.
Frightened, the three girls darted into the
bushes.

It was the Baron! Oh, they hoped he had not seen them.

Those foolish little girls! They fled — across a footbridge and down another path. Ahead they saw a small, wooden shed. The door was standing open.

"Hurry, hurry! Follow me!" cried Dinah. She darted into the shed. Joanne and Suzy followed her. Their hearts pounded wildly.

Oh, if only the Baron had not seen them.

Those foolish little girls!

They crawled into a corner of the shed against some old brooms and rakes and shovels. They clutched one another in fear.

Shh . . . !

Something was rustling the grass outside the shed. Swish . . . swish . . . swish! What was that? Listen, there it was again.

Swish . . . swish . . . swish!

Oh, what could it be? It was close to the door. There it was: a creature! Oh, a strange, hairy creature! It stopped in the doorway and looked inside. It looked straight at them. Oh, and its body was covered with prickly spines. Brr! Suzy screamed in fear. She threw her arms around Dinah's neck and cried, "No, no!

 Mother! Mother!"

And then . . . Then one of the brooms fell over. That scared the girls even more. But — it also scared the prickly creature.

It pulled in its head and raised all its prickles. Oh, it looked so strange, so strange! It looked like a ball stuck full of needles. Brr!

And that horrible creature stayed where it was. It didn't move.

Oh, and now the three sisters could not get out of the shed.

Dinah was the boldest. She hissed, "Kussht! Kussht!" But that terrible creature did not move.

Almost sobbing, Dinah cried, "We have to get out of here, you ugly beast! We have to find our little brother!"

But the terrible creature did not move.

Dinah took two steps forward. "Come on, we'll run past him."

"But what if he bites?" wailed Suzy.

"But what if he pricks us?" wailed Joanne.

Dinah darted through the door. She pulled Suzy along behind her. They slipped past the creature. Then they waited for Joanne.

31

She was afraid. She did not dare.

But . . . zzip! She darted through anyway.

Then they ran away — all three of them.

But they did not know where they were going.

They did not know where Joey was.

And they did not know where the Baron was.

They just ran on and on.

They did not even dare to look back. What if that prickly creature came after them?

Oh, they gasped for breath.

Frrrssh! went the bushes beside them.

The girls jumped in fright. They clutched one another and screamed.

Oh, but it was only a bird. A big bird fluttering up out of the bushes. It had frightened them. But they had also frightened it. Brr! These woods were so dark.

The three girls ran on.

They ran until they could not go another step.

They were tired and sad and frightened.

Suzy's wet shoes went slurp . . . slurp . . . slurp.

And then, suddenly . . . a dog barked nearby.

8. The Baron

Little Joey sat in his wagon, all alone.
Little Joey could not see his sisters, they were gone.
But little Joey did see the delicious, red berries in a corner of the wagon.
He tried to reach them but he couldn't.
A belt held him back.
He stretched out his hand as far as he could.
He became angry at the red berries. "Joey more!" he scolded. "Bad, bad, bad!" The berries were bad because they did not come to him.
Mmm! He could almost taste them. He licked his lips.

Joey was wearing shoes but no socks. One of his shoes had come off. Joey stretched his bare foot into the corner of the wagon.
He reached and reached with his bare little toes.
Yes, oh, yes, he had one. He had a berry under his toes. Quickly he pulled his foot and the berry toward him.
Then he popped the strawberry into his mouth.
Mmm! Good!

He reached for another one . . . and another. Mmm!

Joey forgot his lost sisters. He was much too busy.

And his little toes turned bright red — strawberry red.

Then suddenly . . .

Then Joey heard something. He looked around. Oh, two large hands parted the bushes. Then came a white beard and a black hat. Two large eyes stared at Joey. Those eyes asked a question, "Who are you?"

But Joey was not frightened. He had done nothing wrong. He looked back at the man. His small, happy eyes also asked a question, "Who are you?"

It was . . . it was the Baron.

He had spotted the wagon behind the bushes. That was strange. So he had come for a closer look.

Who was this little boy? How had he gotten here? Was he all alone? How could that be?

He looked like a friendly little boy.

"What's your name?" asked the Baron.

Joey said, "Joey more!" And he popped another strawberry into his mouth.

"Where is your mother?"

Joey said, "Joey more!" And he reached with his toes again. Ah, he had another one.

"How did you get here?"

Joey said, "Joey more!" And he popped another berry into his mouth.

The Baron smiled.

But he was also a little angry. Who had brought the little boy here? Who had picked strawberries for him? Who had put them out of reach in a corner of the wagon?

The Baron began to search.

He searched the paths. He went to the gate.

But he saw no one.

He shouted, "Is anyone here?" No answer.

He muttered, "That's a fine pickle! What shall I do with this little boy? I can't leave him alone in the woods. I can't put him outside the gate. There's no one to look after him."

Joey had eaten all the strawberries and he wanted more. He pointed into the bushes with both hands and cried, "Joey more!" That meant, "Mr. Baron, will you pick me some more of those delicious berries, please?"

But the Baron did not understand.

He muttered, "That's a fine pickle!"

And he pulled the wagon between the bushes and onto the path.

He smiled a little.

He thought, "Won't Nelly be surprised when Grandpa comes home with a little boy!"

9. The Beautiful Garden

Beside the Baron's castle was a large, beautiful garden full of flowers. Beautiful peacocks strutted around showing off their colourful tail feathers. Dozens of goldfish swam in the large pond. In the grass stood little stone angels with baskets full of flowers on their heads. Little stone gnomes lay in the grass laughing at them. Oh, it was a beautiful garden, sparkling with sunshine and colours.

In the middle of the beautiful garden lay a beautiful girl. She lay in a long chair with fine satin pillows behind her back. She wore fine clothes. And on the table stood a silver bowl of cherries.

But the girl's cheeks were very pale and her hands were very thin. She did not look happy at all.

She was sick and she had been sick for a long time. Beside her chair lay a large, strong dog. The girl was petting him. She liked her dog very much. The dog wagged his tail. That meant, "I like you too."

At a little table sat an old lady with silver hair. She looked very grand. She was the Baroness. But she had a friendly smile.

"Grandma . . ."

"Yes, dear."

"I wish I could get up and play."

"I know, dear. But you can't. First you must become stronger."

"But it's taking so long, Grandma!"

"Oh, Nelly, the Lord knows what you need. He knows everything. But you must be patient."

"Yes, Grandma."

"That's good, Nelly. The Lord looks after sick children. You know that."

"Grandma, does the Lord also look after children who aren't sick?"

"Certainly! The Lord looks after everyone, big and . . ."

"Oh, Grandma, look!"

The Baroness put on her glasses. They were gold-rimmed glasses with a gold handle on one side instead of stems. She looked at the woods. The sick girl laughed and the grand old lady laughed too. Look, there came Grandpa. And he was pulling a little wagon. In the wagon sat a little boy. What a funny sight!

Nelly's eyes sparkled with delight. A little boy! Oh, she loved little children. What a cute little boy! With curly hair. "Oh, Grandpa, how cute!

Bring him to me. May he sit on my lap for a little while?"

The Baron looked a little cross. He muttered, "A fine pickle!"
But Nelly looked so delighted that the Baron smiled. And so did the Baroness. They loved Nelly very much.
Nelly said, "Come here, little boy. Come and sit on my lap."
At once Joey held out his arms to Nelly. He saw the shiny red cherries in the bowl on the table. "Joey candy!"
"Oh, Grandma! His foot is bleeding!" Nelly cried shocked.

The Baroness looked at Joey's foot through her fancy glasses. She was also shocked. Yes, his toes were covered with blood.

But the Baron laughed, "Strawberry blood," he said. He carefully lifted Joey out of the wagon. Joey thought he could walk pretty well already. But he couldn't. He took two steps and . . . thump! He sat down on the dog's tail. "Joey go boom!" he cried.
The big dog growled, "What's this sticky little roughneck doing in our nice garden?"

The Baron quickly lifted Joey onto Nelly's lap. And a maid came to wash his toes. Nelly fed him some of the cherries. First she took out the pits.
Joey told her they were very good and that he was having a good time. He bounced up and down on her lap. "Joey more! Joey more candy!" He held out a pit to the dog.
Nelly's cheeks glowed with delight. He was such a cute little boy! "Grandpa, is he going to stay with us? Oh, that would be fun!"
"I'm afraid not, Nelly. He belongs to someone else. But I don't know who. He was left alone in the woods. His mother must be worried about

him. I wonder who brought him into the woods? I did not see anyone. We will have to find out who he belongs to. I guess we will have to take him to the police station."

"To the police station? Oh, no! Will they put him in jail?" Nelly hugged Joey tightly. "No!" Grandma laughed. So did Grandpa.

But the dog began to growl. He lifted his head and pricked up his ears. He listened. Suddenly he jumped up. He heard something. "Woof-woof!" He dashed through the garden toward the woods. "Woof-woof!"

What did he hear?

10. The Whole Story

Listen! What was *that!*
The big dog dashed into the dark woods.
"Woof-woof!"
Suddenly screams and shrieks rang out in the woods.
Oh, what *was* that?
The Baron cried, "Here, boy! Come back here!"

He hurried after the dog. The gardener also ran up.

The Baroness watched them through her fancy glasses. Joey listened. He held up his hand and said, "Doggy say woof-woof!"

Nelly looked startled. "Oh, Grandma, look!"

Out of the woods came the three foolish sisters. They walked between the Baron and the gardener. Behind them walked the big dog.

They walked toward Grandma and Nelly, crying with fear. Dinah's apron was torn. Joanne's nose was red with strawberry blood. And Suzy had wiped away her tears with her muddy handkerchief. So her cheeks were black. None of the girls dared to look up. They were too frightened. The big dog had scared them horribly and so had the Baron and the gardener.

But the Baron was smiling a little. And the Baroness said kindly, "Oh, poor dears!"

And Joey shouted, "Joey! Joey candy!" That meant, "Come on! I've been here a long time already. They have berries here too — even better than those in the woods."

The three girls heard his voice. "There's Joey! There's Joey!" Oh, how happy they were! They smiled through their tears.

Suzy ran to Joey. She forgot the Baron. She forgot the Baroness. She forgot everyone. She had eyes only for her little brother. He was back safe. Joey was back!

But then they had to tell the whole story to the Baroness. "Oh, such foolish sisters!" she said. "You should not have left your little brother all alone. That was wrong!"

"Yes ma'am," sniffed Dinah.

"It made you sad and frightened, didn't it? That's what happens when you do something wrong. Will you look after your little brother from now on?"

"Yes, ma'am," sniffed the three sisters.

Nelly looked a little sad. She called her Grandpa to her. She threw her arm around his neck and whispered something in his ear. With her other arm she held Joey. Look at him. Laughing, he pushed his face into the Baron's beard. He giggled as it tickled him. "Joey tickle!"

The Baron did not mind. "Yes, I'll do it," he whispered to Nelly. Then he said, "Listen, you foolish little girls, this girl wants to *keep* your little brother. She says she can look after him better than you can. Is that all right with you?"
"Oh, no, Mr. Baron!" they all cried, shocked.
The Baron laughed. "I was only teasing. He is your little brother and you had better take him home to his mother.

"But listen — you may all come back tomorrow. All right? Then you can pick strawberries in the woods again. This time the gardener will not chase you away. And Nelly will look after Joey while you  are in the woods. She likes little children. All right?"
"Yes, Mr. Baron!" the three girls said happily.
"Oh, yes, Grandpa!" cried Nelly happily.
"All right!" said the Baron. "Now it's time for you to be on your way home."

Off they went.

Dinah and Joanne pulled the wagon and Suzy pushed. Little Joey cried, "Joey go fast! Joey ride!"

Through the big iron gate they went. First they walked. Then they went faster. At last they were running. Home to Mother!

11. Good Night

It was night.

Nelly lay in her fine bed. Grandma sat beside her.

"Go to sleep now, Nelly. Tomorrow will soon be here."

"Yes, Grandma. Oh, won't it be fun?"

"See? I told you, Nelly. The Lord looks after sick children. He has made you happy. Will you be patient now? And will you go to sleep?"

"Yes, Grandma." Nelly folded her hands and said her bedtime prayers. She was very thankful.

The three foolish little sisters were also lying in bed. Mother was sitting beside them. Joey was already sleeping.

"First say your prayers and then go right to sleep. Tomorrow will soon be here."

"Yes, Mother, yes!" they bubbled with joy.

"What if Joey were still in those dark woods? Oh, it makes me shiver to think of it. But the Lord was looking after you — after all of you. Did you know that?"

"Yes, Mother," they said softly. Then they knelt

beside their pillows and said their bedtime prayers. They were very thankful.

And in the hole in the old wall four little birds also settled down for the night. They were tucked warmly under their father and mother's wings. Little brother was back home too. His father and mother had found him. They had showed him how to get back: under the gate, onto a little tree, then onto a bigger one, and then onto the wall.
Now they were all fast asleep.

Above the wall towered the dark trees.
Beyond them hung the dark sky.
And beyond the sky is Heaven.
That is where the Lord lives, Who looks after all His creatures.
The little birds did not know that.
But the little children did.

Titles in this series: